Can I Come Too?

For Billy Kiddle —B. P.

For Bun and Bees —N. B.

Published by
PEACHTREE PUBLISHERS
1700 Chattahoochee Avenue
Atlanta, Georgia 30318-2112
www.peachtree-online.com

Text © 2013 by Brian Patten
Illustrations © 2013 by Nicola Bayley

First published in Great Britain in 2013 by Andersen Press Ltd.
First United States version published in 2014 by Peachtree Publishers

Design and composition by Nicola Carmack and Melanie McMahon Ives
The illustrations were rendered in colored pencil on cartridge paper.

Printed in April 2014 by Tien Wah Press in Malaysia
10 9 8 7 6 5 4 3 2 1
First Edition

Library of Congress Cataloging-in-Publication Data

Patten, Brian, 1946-
Can I come too? / Brian Patten ; illustrated by Nicola Bayley.
pages cm
ISBN: 978-1-56145-796-0
Summary: A mouse leads a group of animals on a search for the biggest creature in the world.
[1. Mice—Fiction. 2. Animals—Fiction. 3. Size—Fiction.] I. Bayley, Nicola, illustrator. II. Title.
PZ7.P2757Can 2014
[E]—dc23
2013045420

Can I Come Too?

Brian Patten & Nicola Bayley

PEACHTREE

ATLANTA

A very small mouse decided she
wanted to have a very big adventure.
*I'll go and find the biggest creature
in the world*, she thought.

By the lake, the mouse met a frog. "Are you the biggest creature in the world?" she asked.

"No," said the frog. "But it is very brave of you to look for it. Can I come too?"

"Of course," said the mouse. "Just because we are small doesn't mean we can't have a big adventure."

On a branch overhanging the river, they met
a bird made out of rainbows. It was a kingfisher.

"Are you the biggest creature in the world?"
the mouse asked.

"I'm a rather small bird," he said, "but I'd love
to see what the biggest creature is. Can I come too?"

Dozing on a wall in the sunlight was a cat.
"Have you seen the biggest creature
in the world?" the mouse asked.
The cat opened an eye and said, "No, but
I'm curious to see it. I'll come too."

They met an otter on the riverbank where the wildflowers grew.

"Perhaps you are the biggest creature in the world," said the mouse.

"I'm afraid not," said the otter, "but I wonder what is? Can I come too?"

In the woods, where everything glowed with a green light, they met a badger. "Are you the biggest creature in the world?" the mouse asked.

"His legs are far too short to belong to the biggest creature," sniffed the cat.

"But I'd love to see what it is," said the badger. "Can I come too?"

They crossed a little bridge in a small valley full of tiny things. Dragonflies darted around, lizards lazed on stones, and a water vole washed his whiskers at the river's edge. But they saw nothing big.

So on they went.

When they met a dog, the mouse asked,
"Are you the biggest creature in the world?"
The cat said, "He's the scruffiest creature,
but he's certainly not the biggest."
And the dog said, "I wonder
what on earth is?
Can I come too?"

Halfway up the
mountainside, they
met a goat. "Have you
seen the biggest creature
in the world?" asked the mouse.
"No, but I can see some very large
creatures from up here in this tree," she said.
"Well, we're looking for the biggest of
them all," said the mouse.
And the goat said, "Can I come too?"

In the zoo, they met a tiger.
Her paws were as big as frying pans.

"You're the most fantastic creature
in the world!" declared the mouse.
Perhaps you are also the biggest."

"I'm not the biggest," said the tiger.
"If I promise not to eat anyone, can
I come too?"

The polar bear followed them out of the zoo. His coat was as white as snow. "I believe the biggest creature in the world lives in the ocean where the river ends," he said. "I'd love to see it. Can I come too?"

So off they went.

The mouse, the frog, the kingfisher, the cat, the otter, the badger, the dog, the goat, the tiger, and the polar bear followed the river to the ocean.

The mouse was very excited. *I wonder what we're going to see?* she thought.

The biggest creature was something
as big as an island. Something bigger
than a million mice. Seagulls flew
above it. Dolphins leapt around it.

It
was a
WHALE!

The animals watched until the whale plunged back beneath the waves. Then night fell, and all the sleepy creatures decided it was time to go back home.

"We would never have seen such a wonderful thing without you," they said to the little mouse.

And the little mouse said, "Meeting you has been a very big part of the adventure. I'm so glad you all could come too."

The mouse was so happy to have seen the biggest creature in the world. That night she thought to herself, *I might be tiny, but I've had a very big adventure.*

And then she curled up into a little ball and fell fast asleep.